Bumble Bugs and Elephants

A Big and Little Book

Bumble Bugs and Elephants: A Big and Little Book
Copyright 1938 by Margaret Wise Brown. Copyright renewed 1966 by Roberta Brown Rauch
New illustrations copyright © 2006 by Thacher Hurd
Manufactured in China.
For information address HarperCollins Children's Books, a division of HarperCollins Publishers,
1350 Avenue of the Americas, New York, NY 10019.
www.harperchildrens.com

Library of Congress Cataloging-in-Publication Data
Brown, Margaret Wise, 1910–1952
    Bumble bugs and elephants : a big and little book / by Margaret Wise Brown ; pictures by Clement
Hurd.
        p.   cm.
    Summary: Great big and tiny little animals interact side by side.
    ISBN-10: 0-06-074512-6 — ISBN-10: 0-06-074513-4 (lib. bdg.)
    ISBN-13: 978-0-06-074512-7 — ISBN-13: 978-0-06-074513-4 (lib. bdg.)
    1. Animals—Juvenile fiction. [1. Animals—Fiction. 2. Size—Fiction.] I. Hurd, Clement, 1908– ill. II.
Title.
PZ10.3.B7656Bum 2006   2004030195
[E]—dc22   CIP
                                                                                                AC

Typography by Elynn Cohen   1 2 3 4 5 6 7 8 9 10   ❖   First Edition

Bumble Bugs and Elephants

A Big and Little Book

By Margaret Wise Brown

Pictures by Clement Hurd

HarperCollins*Publishers*

Once upon a time
there was a great big bumble bug

and a tiny little bumble bug

And there was
a great big butterfly

and a little tiny butterfly

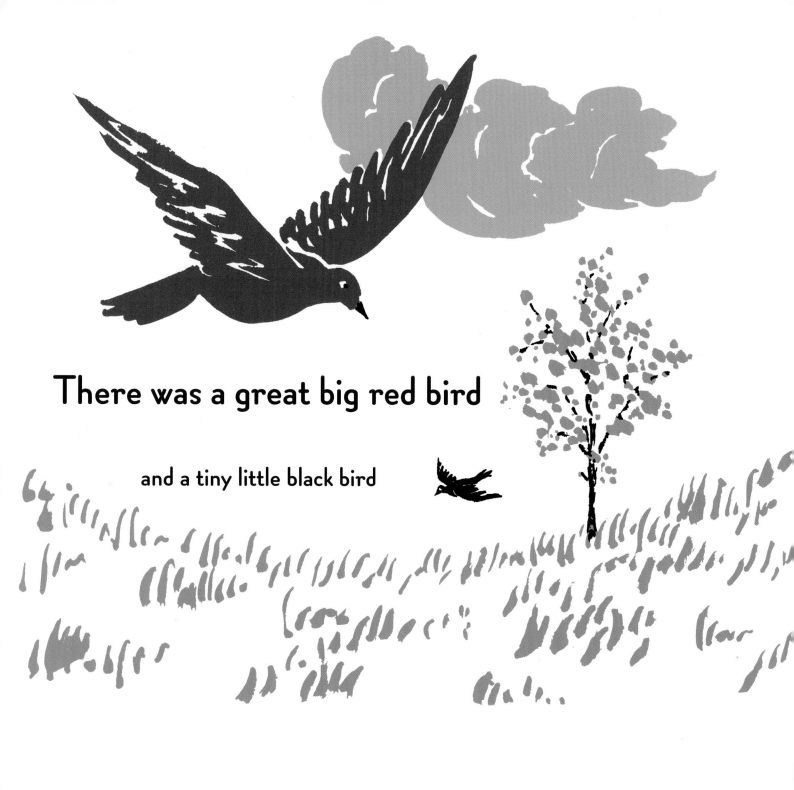

There was a great big red bird

and a tiny little black bird

And a little tiny turtle   and a great big turtle

There were two great big chickens

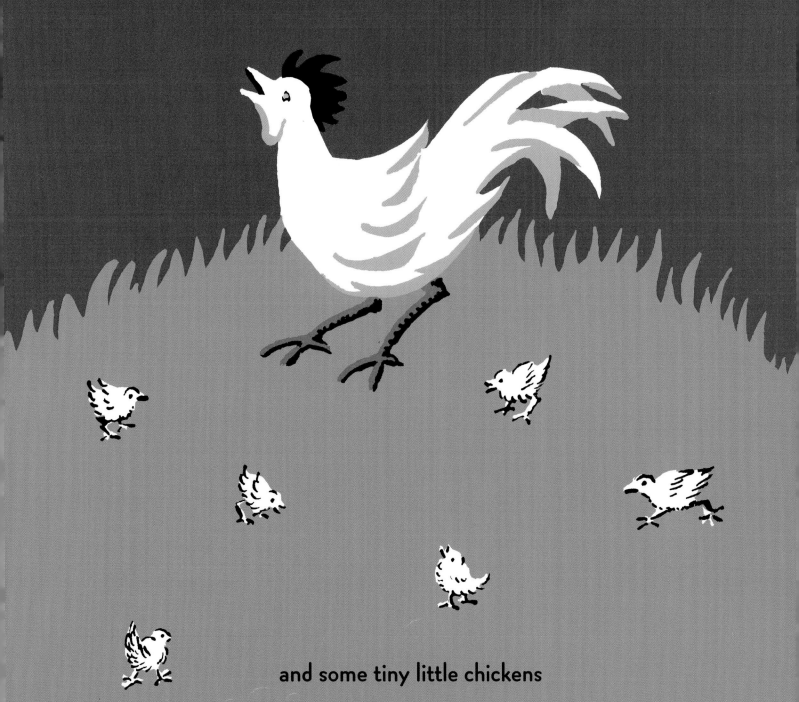

and some tiny little chickens

There were some great big fish

and a lot of little fish

There were two little dogs

and a great big dog

There were three little pigs

and a great big pig

A little tiny horse

and a great big horse

And there was a
great big elephant

and a little tiny elephant

What do you know

that is great big?

What do you know that is tiny little?

Once upon a time
there was a great big bumble bug . . .